NOT HERE TO MAKE YOU COMFORTABLE

NOT HERE TO MAKE YOU COMFORTABLE

50 WOMEN WHO
STAND UP. SPEAK OUT. INSPIRE CHANGE.

'The duty we owe ourselves is greater than that we owe others.'

Louisa May Alcott, author of Little Women

Preface

In January 2022, activist and author Grace Tame did not smile at a reception with the then prime minister of Australia. Her face was splashed across newspapers and online and, in a matter of minutes, people were discussing and dissecting her demeanour.

It got us – women working in Young Readers publishing – talking about how unforgivingly scrutinised women are for their appearance and behaviour.

We have all been told to 'Smile!' by a stranger as we passed by with our face set in an indifferent expression. Imagine heading to work or school with your mind full of thoughts about last night's episode of your favourite podcast, your to-do list for the day and how many metres you are from your favourite cafe. You haven't been thinking about how your face might appear to anyone else, and as for the guy who thought it necessary to chirp in from the periphery of your vision – you hadn't been thinking about him at all.

But why does a random on the street feel entitled to command a smile, and it is on us to sidestep him? Why are women's faces still constantly, *tirelessly* policed by society? Furthermore, why is a cheery countenance so damn important? What if, instead of distracted indifference, we charge past him in anger? With irrepressible, bubbling rage? Is our anger any more his business than our happiness? It is not incumbent on us to make a stranger feel better about his day, or to take notes on how we should feel about our day from him.

Few would admit to siding with this guy, but people were more than happy to pile onto Grace Tame's apparent disregard for the feelings of those around her.

Like yellow cars, once we had observed Grace Tame's honest expression we couldn't help noticing examples of women's courage everywhere. From Taylor Swift's unparalleled boss move of rerecording her back catalogue to young activists holding politicians accountable; from Nadya Okamoto's taboo-breaking imagery of menstruation to Hannah Gadsby's heartbreaking honesty about trauma: we were, and continue to be, inspired by women who challenge gendered behavioural expectations and are simply their authentic selves.

And it's not just famous people. Every day we are inspired by young people who are spirited and thoughtful; brave and funny; determined and vulnerable. As with every project we do, this book is both inspired by and for the people reading it.

Lots has been written on emotional honesty. Being bold and true to yourself should not look like aggression or nasty put-downs in the name of 'honesty'. But it does look like being honest with yourself. It can look like:

Saying no to something you don't want to do.

Standing up for a friend.

Having boundaries and holding them.

Choosing to not answer a question you're uncomfortable answering.

Standing strong and brushing off criticism.

Feeling free to get things wrong and try again.

Wearing what you want with scant regard for so-called fashion.

Speaking your mind instead of kowtowing to the opinions of others.

This book isn't a manifesto of anger, even if we have plenty to be angry about. It's a celebration of assertiveness and certitude. It's about taking risks and finding your courage.

It's easy to focus so hard on behaving like an adult that we can forget what it was like to be young. Small children have many traits, including, importantly, candour. They burst into tears when they're upset, furrow their brows when they're angry, squeal with unbridled joy when they're happy. They know how they're feeling and they let us know pretty clearly too. Being authentic leads to connection, respect, empathy. It's a gift we sometimes forget to embrace, but we don't have to outgrow it.

This book will, we hope, go some small way to contributing to a society where people do not feel entitled to weigh in on our faces.

- Penguin Random House Australia

Contents

Here are fifty times a woman did something exceptional.

We saw you.

Reflecting on these moments – some were acts of quiet courage, others of heroic magnitude – inspired us to be more confident in being true to ourselves.

It's time to stop saying yes to everything.

It's time to stop apologising unnecessarily.

It's time to stop avoiding conflict at all costs.

It's time to be true to our emotions, whatever they are.

And if time makes a moment, and a collection of moments makes a movement, our collective acts of certitude can help create a fairer and truer society.

We're not here to make you comfortable.

We're here to be ourselves.

There was that time a young woman *picked up a microphone* and called herself

A.GIRL.

And she took on the stage and radio waves.

And she was talented and brilliant and unafraid to sing about where she was from.

And she didn't try to glamorise or delete her truth. She spoke out about fear, injustice and trauma, and she showed that pain can coexist with beauty.

And in doing so she brought the outside in.

A.Girl's songs explore the realities of life in the western suburbs of Sydney, an area often unfairly stereotyped in media imagery.

She is bold and unapologetic in her lyrics, and through her music she reaches out to those who may feel unseen or unvalued.

She advocates for more creative opportunities for women from western Sydney.

A.Girl stands for unity and love rather than division and competition.

There was that time

YASSMIN ABDEL-MAGIED

was the only girl in her high school woodwork class and

was on the receiving end of jibes and jeers

from not only her peers but her teacher.

And still, she showed up. At the gym, where she could bench-press as much as the lads. And at university, when she was not a common sight as a hijab-wearing woman in her Engineering degree.

And she spoke up about the plight of those who are oppressed and was met with threats of violence and death.

And the point she was making was lost, because she was held to a standard unfairly placed on women, especially women who do not fit a particular Anglo paradigm.

Yassmin Abdel-Magied is an activist, author and mechanical engineer.

She was Queensland's Young Australian of the Year in 2015 for her community work, and 2018's recipient of the Young Voltaire Award for being a role model to young women, Muslims and migrants. She is the author of four books and at age sixteen she founded Youth Without Borders, a youth-led organisation.

Yassmin Abdel-Magied is brilliant, courageous in her activism and uncompromising in her rejection of racism, sexism and bigotry.

Illustrated by
Rebecca King

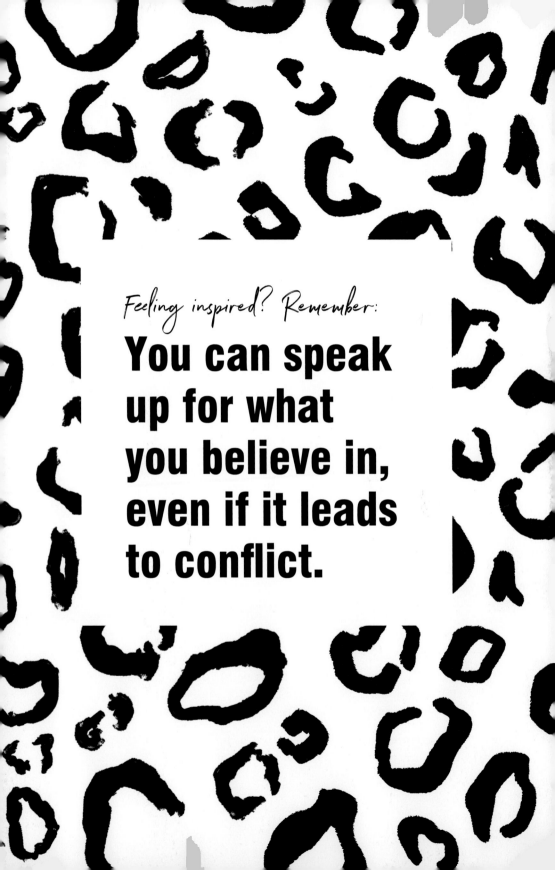

Feeling inspired? Remember:

You can speak up for what you believe in, even if it leads to conflict.

There was that time a writer

CHIMAMANDA NGOZI ADICHIE

started a global conversation about

strength and *freedom* and *stories*.

And people found her provocative because she pushed for writers to speak the truth in literature and in life regardless of whether it caused discomfort.

And others objected to the way her words about feminism started to shape a younger generation of women, but she kept speaking them anyway.

Chimamanda Ngozi Adichie was born and raised in Nigeria. She moved to the United States and holds a degree in Communication and Political Science, a Master's Degree in Creative Writing from Johns Hopkins University and a Master of Arts degree in African History from Yale University.

She has written fiction and non-fiction books, and her TED Talks on feminism, writing and under-representation have gone global.

Her book *We Should All Be Feminists* was distributed to every sixteen-year-old school student in Sweden, to promote gender equality as a cornerstone of society.

In 2015, Chimamanda was named one of *TIME* magazine's 100 Most Influential People in the World and, in 2017, *Fortune* magazine named her one of the World's 50 Greatest Leaders.

Chimamanda Ngozi Adichie shows us how to speak and write our own truth.

Illustrated by
Violet Tobacco

There was that time

EVELYN ARALUEN

spoke out about unceded

land and let her *fury* show.

And she spoke up about the systemic barriers to a fair and just nation.

And she wasn't afraid to take on the establishment even when – especially when – it was difficult to hear.

And she called out several Australian literary classics, and refused to allow Aboriginal presence on Aboriginal land be erased.

And she was courageous and relentless in her advocacy, which made people uncomfortable.

And her writing continues to confront the iconography of an unreconciled nation, using satire and humour alongside anger.

Evelyn Araluen is a descendant of the Bundjalung nation, a writer, educator and editor who advocates for better funding for artists and writers and continues to engage in the conversation about her native land.

She is passionate about books and storytelling and advocates for increased representation of First Nations voices in traditional book publishing.

She is fascinated by the stories of women and gender diverse writers who tell their truths to share their lived experiences.

Evelyn Araluen is strong and articulate and not afraid to speak loudly.

Illustrated by
Tori-Jay Mordey

There was that time a *smart* and *funny* woman

CELESTE BARBER

played the internet

at its own game.

And she danced and played and wore whatever she wanted, and we all laughed and connected and felt a bit better about our perceived imperfections.

And she reminded us that we don't have to be the same body shape or have the same hair colour or hide ourselves away. We can be exactly who we are and be loved for it. And we can love ourselves.

Celeste Barber is an actor and a writer and a comedian and a beloved Australian. She shines a light on the absurdity of the expectations pop culture places on women to be a particular size and shape, and she says what the hell.

She used her celebrity status to raise AU$51 million for victims of Australia's 2020 bushfires.

She still dances and plays, spreading fun and warmth wherever she goes, showing us that we too can do whatever we want.

Celeste Barber is smart and funny and compassionate and kind – and much more.

Illustrated by
Georgia Perry

There was that time an athlete

ASH BARTY

shocked the tennis world and

quit at the top of her game.

And people around the world asked: Why? Why wouldn't she keep going until she held the most records and had the most wins and was considered the best there ever was?

And, at age twenty-five and ranked number one in the world, she retired from professional tennis after winning three Grand Slams, showing us that success is whatever you want it to be. The path you take in life is yours to choose, not what anyone else dictates.

Ash Barty is a hugely talented sportswoman, finding success on the tennis court and the cricket pitch.

She has won the French Open, Wimbledon and the Australian Open and represented her country at the Tokyo Olympics, and is the National Indigenous Tennis Ambassador for Tennis Australia. She is also an ambassador for RSPCA Queensland.

She advocates for the next generation of sports lovers, particularly Indigenous kids like she was.

Ash Barty is an inspiration and exactly who she wants to be.

Illustrated by
Janelle Burger

Passive =
Letting others decide for you.

Aggressive =
Deciding for others.

ASSERTIVE =
Deciding for *yourself*.

There was that time that was the worst time
any of us could have ever imagined, and

GLADYS BEREJIKLIAN

was *thrust into the*
daily spotlight.

And as state premier of New South Wales she was not afraid to
show up. For many months during the Covid-19 pandemic, she
appeared for live television updates and interviews almost every
day: a vulnerable approach rarely conducted by politicians.

And when she made decisions that were unpopular she stood
her ground, showing stoicism and self-belief. Equally, when she
changed her position on earlier decisions she showed guts.

And as she weathered personal attacks and fastidious scrutiny and
higher accountability than many male counterparts, still she backed
herself and was not afraid to be disliked.

Gladys Berejiklian was the premier of New South Wales during
two of the biggest crises in recent history: the Black Summer
bushfires and the Covid-19 pandemic. She was on the ground
beside the fire chief as the state burned, and during the
pandemic she made difficult decisions that had to evolve
and adapt with the developing situation.

She did not get everything right.

She was determined and ambitious and imperfect.

Gladys Berejiklian showed us how to persist. How to show
up and stand up.

There was that time a world-champion gymnast

SIMONE BILES

shocked the world when she withdrew from the 2020 Olympic Games finals in order to

prioritise her mental health.

And by doing so she shone a light on the topic of athletes' mental health and shook up the sporting community. Since then, many other sportspeople have followed her lead.

And she demonstrated that looking after yourself – on all levels – is key to being a well-rounded and happy human being.

And she didn't persist at all costs.

And she valued herself.

Simone Biles is the most decorated gymnast in US history. She has won 32 medals, and her skill, courage and innovation have resulted in at least four skills being named after her.

Her domination of the gymnastics world and dedication to the sport contributed to an increase in other gymnasts of colour training and excelling around the United States.

Simone Biles is a legend and leader in her field, and an amazing advocate for women around the world.

Illustrated by
Sabrena Khadija

Feeling inspired? Remember:

Honesty is a sign of courage.

There was that time a young actor

MILLIE BOBBY BROWN

fought back against the media

and the online trolls who tried

to sexualise her and force her to

'come of age' before she was ready.

And she reclaimed her voice by deleting her social media accounts and allowed herself to enter adulthood at her own pace, in her own way.

And she didn't give in to the pressure to be someone she wasn't.

And she challenged us to view her as a person, not property.

Millie Bobby Brown rose to fame at age twelve when she played the role of Eleven in the cult hit series *Stranger Things*. At age fourteen she became the youngest ever UNICEF Goodwill Ambassador, campaigning for children's rights worldwide.

She was a child actor and now she is forging her career as an adult, making her own choices.

She is learning to navigate life like all young women must.

Millie Bobby Brown is talented and famous and in control of her life.

There was that time a young, blind

NAS CAMPANELLA

dreamed of becoming a journalist

and *refused* to let her disability stop her.

And when she walked into job interviews with her cane, plenty of people told her she couldn't possibly be a journalist.

And Nas persevered, backing herself and owning her strengths.

And she knew she deserved a career that celebrated her merit and her skills.

Nas Campanella became the ABC's first blind cadet journalist in 2011 and has continued to chase – and achieve – her career goals, working for a decade for the ABC as a regional reporter and finding success as a radio newsreader, presenter and senior producer.

She is currently the ABC's National Disability Affairs Reporter, appearing on national television, radio and online to report on important topics such as the Disability Royal Commission.

She is an ambassador for the Australian Human Rights Commission's IncludeAbility campaign and was named Disability Confident Changemaker of the Year by the Australian Network on Disability.

Nas Campanella works to elevate the voices of people with disability and to advocate for change.

Illustrated by
Sabrena Khadija

Did you know . . .

Women use phrases like:

> **'I think . . .'**

> **'Just . . .'**

> **'Only . . .'**

> **'Actually . . .'**

. . . a lot more often than men do.

Often we don't even realise we use these verbal modifiers
to come across as friendly and non-confrontational.

These qualifiers can make us come across as uncertain, or
underqualified to speak on a topic, even when we are neither.

Small tweaks to our language can be all it takes to avoid this.

For example:

'I think we could perhaps consider a different direction, just in
case the first idea doesn't work out. Does that make sense?' versus
'Let's consider a different direction too. What do you think?'

You can communicate with warmth and friendliness (A warm greeting!
A thoughtful compliment!) and still know your stuff.

There was that time a teenage

AJ CLEMENTINE

shared her gender affirmation journey with the world,

helping people who share similar experiences

feel *supported* and *seen*.

And she used her platform to speak on her mixed-race Asian and trans identity, and about the bullying and ostracism she experienced.

And she fostered a loving, safe space for her community, simultaneously educating and raising awareness.

And she showed us that sharing and listening to authentic stories will help not only trans people but anyone who feels like they don't fit in and is looking for somewhere to belong.

AJ Clementine is a TikTok sensation, model, writer and influencer. She is a trans and LGBTQIA+ ally, and her content has captivated millions of people.

She was the first trans model for the staple Australian brand BONDS, and has partnerships with ubiquitous labels such as Pandora, Disney, Australis and Mecca. Her book, *Girl Transcending*, speaks on her journey of navigating self-love and acceptance as a trans woman – then and now.

AJ Clementine is resilient and courageous, breaking stereotypes and affirming trans experiences.

Illustrated by
Rebecca King

There was that time a student

CHANEL CONTOS

created an online survey that *asked girls the question*:
Who has been sexually harassed or assaulted
during their school years?

And young women replied. In the thousands. Detailing their abuse and the toxic environment of predominantly all-boys schools across Sydney.

And the survey exploded. Girls raised their voices and told their stories.

And people in power had to sit up and take notice and talk about how boys are being raised and the power imbalance between the genders. As a result, law-makers and educators re-examined the way consent education was handled in Australian schools. But there is still more work to be done, and Chanel is leading the way.

Chanel Contos founded Teach Us Consent, which lobbies for schools to provide holistic consent and sexuality education, calling on NSW schools to start teaching consent earlier and include lessons on rape culture, slut-shaming, sexual coercion, toxic masculinity, victim blaming, enthusiastic consent and queer sex.

She was not prepared to let girls continue to be harassed and assaulted, or for boys to grow up not understanding the full nature of consent.

She is still working to continue this conversation. At the time of print, NSW Education had not made changes to its consent education.

Chanel Contos is a young woman who asked a question and started a vital conversation.

EACH TIME A WOMAN
STANDS UP
for herself,
WITHOUT KNOWING IT POSSIBLY,
WITHOUT *Claiming* IT,
SHE STANDS UP FOR
ALL WOMEN

MAYA ANGELOU

RACHEL CUSK

wrote honestly about motherhood and

was forced to *defend her truth.*

And her book *A Life's Work* shared, with unflinching honesty, her experience of parenthood. It wasn't all babycinos and vintage daybeds. Rachel was real and she was tired and she loved her children and her writing was moving and startling and funny and true.

And when the book was released she was harshly criticised by many readers and media outlets, not as a writer but as a mother because she didn't present a honeyed, wholesome and happy version of mothering.

And her book made people uncomfortable, showing the unfair expectations on women to shoulder the enormous weight of child-rearing while being stymied from speaking honestly about its difficulties.

Rachel Cusk is an award-winning author and writer living in the United Kingdom. Her writing has been described as 'landmark' and *A Life's Work* is lauded for its accuracy when describing the experience of early parenthood.

She demonstrated that it is possible for love and exhaustion to coexist – it is not an either-or situation.

Rachel Cusk showed us the strength in believing your own story.

There was that time a musician

BILLIE EILISH

made young people realise that being

themselves is okay. *More than okay.*

And she wrote music and made songs that said what she wanted to say rather than what people told her she should say.

And she styled herself for herself, not for other people, embracing loose, gender-neutral clothing in order to not allow other people to judge her body, like so many young women are judged.

Billie Eilish is one of the most successful singer-songwriters of her generation. When she was thirteen, she wrote a song called 'Ocean Eyes' for her dance teacher – she didn't plan for the world to hear it, but it did. And then some.

She was the youngest artist (and second in history) to win the top four Grammy awards in one year, 2020: Best New Artist, Song of the Year, Record of the Year and Album of the Year.

She speaks out about issues that are important to her, including encouraging young people to vote, and for American women to have access to safe, legal abortion.

She released her debut album in March 2019, and she keeps going strong.

Billie Eilish is who she is, and you can be too.

Illustrated by
Janelle Burger

STOP Asking Yourself IF YOU'RE GOOD ENOUGH FOR PEOPLE. ARE THEY EVEN Good Enough FOR YOU?

— FLORENCE GIVEN —

There was that time a young activist

CAITLIN FIGUEIREDO

started to *shape the future*

of Australian politics.

And she went to the United Nations and to the White House and to Buckingham Palace on her journey of advocacy to show that we all have a voice, no matter our background, our age or our gender.

And she reminded us that inclusion, safety and diversity are key to our future, delivering her message that politics isn't for the elite, it's about communities choosing their representation.

And she set an example that all girls can follow: no matter where you come from, you can make a difference.

Caitlin Figueiredo was the 2018 ACT Young Woman of the Year and is the youngest entrant on Australia's 100 most influential women's list.

She was named a Global Changemaker for Gender Equality in 2016 at the United State of Women summit in Washington, which she attended at the invitation of the then US First Lady, Michelle Obama.

She founded Jasiri Australia, a program that encourages young female political thinkers to strive for a life of leadership. Among its initiatives is #GirlsTakeOverParliament, which sees young women go into Parliament to see how its occupants really work.

Caitlin Figueiredo believes that all voices count and should be heard, and that everybody has the ability to change the world.

There was that time

CARLY FINDLAY

challenged people to be more *inclusive*.

And she placed herself visibly in the media to challenge harmful and ignorant reporting of people with facial difference and other disabilities.

And challenging public perceptions made her a target for online vitriol and abuse.

And given that she suffers from the rare skin condition ichthyosis, she knows just how much representation matters. She shares her own lived experiences, and through her work in the field of disability she has made the society we live in a better, kinder and more inclusive place.

Carly Findlay received a medal of the Order of Australia for her advocacy work for people with disabilities. Her memoir, *Say Hello*, was published in 2019 and she works as a writer, speaker and appearance advocate.

She won't be defined by other people.

She will advocate for those who need a voice.

Carly Findlay is proud of her identity and helps others to feel the same way about themselves.

TURNING OFF
NOTIFICATIONS

$$=$$

SELF-CARE

OFF

CLEMENTINE FORD

*got angry and **refused to be silenced**.*

And she wrote about what made her angry, and she kept writing and calling out behaviour that made her angry. About gender inequality and violence against women and efforts to keep girls quiet.

And she refused to stop, even as she endured threats from the people perpetrating the behaviour she was calling out.

And she was labelled a 'man hater' and an 'angry feminist', and she showed us that staying quiet, playing nice, like girls are often told to do, is not the way forward.

And she continues to speak up.

Clementine Ford is a feminist writer, broadcaster and public speaker. She has spent decades shining a critical light on issues such as men's violence towards women, rape culture and gender inequality in Australia.

She refuses to stay silent.

She refuses to play nice.

She fights. Like a girl.

Clementine Ford is loud, proud and uncompromising, and unapologetic about her anger.

There was that time an Australian comedian

HANNAH GADSBY

got the whole world talking with her *searing,* *honest* and *angry* Netflix special *Nanette*.

And she changed comedy forever by brilliantly dissecting and laying bare all of comedy's tricks and tools – all while using them in the show to make us laugh.

And by talking so candidly about trauma, gender and sexuality she made us realise that not all punchlines are funny.

Hannah Gadsby's *Nanette* was the definition of uncomfortable – she made us laugh, then told us why we shouldn't. We all learned something when we watched *Nanette*. When Hannah said she was quitting comedy, what she was really quitting was internalised shame, internalised misogyny, all the ways she'd been held back, bullied and tormented, all the ways she thought she 'had' to be to fit in. Hannah was ready to roar. And she did.

She went on to produce another worldwide sold-out show and Netflix special, *Douglas*, in which she talks about what it's like to be diagnosed with autism as an adult, and she's written a bestselling memoir, *Ten Steps to Nanette*.

She has shone a spotlight on so many things that need attention and made people want to discuss them.

Hannah Gadsby is self-deprecating, angry, funny and no longer willing to be silent.

I DON'T WANT TO

UNITE

YOU WITH

Laughter

OR

ANGER.

I JUST NEED MY

STORY

HEARD.

HANNAH GADSBY

There was that time a young woman

KHADIJA GBLA

got *angry*.

And she was told not to shine, that no man would want to marry her if she was too smart or too outspoken.

And she saw this unfair expectation for what it was: a societal dismissal of a woman's valid emotions, and a culture not conducive to meeting a woman's needs.

And she channelled her anger into productivity and strategy.

And her words cut through and resonated, and she gave a voice to an estimated 200,000 Australian girls and women who may have experienced the practice known as female genital mutilation. She didn't hide away from a topic that is shocking and confronting – and in doing so, she is activating change.

Khadija Gbla is an African Australian feminist and human rights activist. She was born in Sierra Leone and spent her younger years in Gambia before arriving in Australia as a refugee at age thirteen.

She is a cultural consultant and inspirational speaker, and through her advocacy organisation No FGM Australia she leads the fight against female genital mutilation.

Khadija Gbla is an inspiration to all.

There was that time an Australian
Lebanese journalist turned filmmaker

DAIZY GEDEON

decided that *enough was enough*

and turned her lens to the top.

And she asked the questions other people were too afraid to ask.

And she created a documentary portraying the problems facing Lebanon, the country of her birth.

And she advocated for truth and change and she had the courage to believe that the people of Lebanon deserved better.

Daizy Gedeon is a filmmaker whose documentary *Enough! Lebanon's Darkest Hour* explores the power, corruption and mismanagement of the country's governing elite. She was praised for the documentary but also warned that discussing Lebanon's politics so publicly could have dangerous repercussions for her. Long-time friends withdrew their public support for the film out of fear.

She reported on international issues as a journalist, and now she is advocating to fix them.

She is brave and bold and tireless in her advocacy.

She connects with people, and she seeks the truth. A journalist never stops asking questions.

Daizy Gedeon shows us what we can do if we listen.

Illustrated by
Michelle Pereira

**Dutch people are less likely to say sorry than people
from other countries. (sbs.com.au)**
They tend to have a straightforward communication style where people
say what they mean and expect others to do the same. Excessive politeness
can be viewed with suspicion, because it could suggest the speaker isn't
being direct or forthcoming.

There was that time the then prime minister of Australia

JULIA GILLARD

called out the leader of the Opposition for his hypocrisy in accusing a member of her party of sexism and misogyny.

And she said:

> I will not be lectured about sexism
> and misogyny by this man.
> I will not.
>
> And the Government will not be lectured
> about sexism and misogyny by this man.
> Not now, not ever.

And the video clip and transcript of her speech went viral worldwide.

And has since inspired multiple take-downs, TikToks and T-shirts.

And encouraged women to call out toxic behaviour in others.

Julia Gillard was Australia's 27th prime minister and the first – and, to date, the only – woman to hold the office. Public criticism of her was not limited to her party's policies as was the case for the men who went before her, but included scathing comments on her body, her clothing and her family, highlighting the unfair evaluation of women in the public eye.

On occasion, Julia Gillard was brought to tears in parliament, including when she introduced legislation to help fund the National Disability Insurance Scheme. Seeing a leader show vulnerability can be empowering and is an example of the advantages of displaying emotions that have historically been associated with women. Tears are not a sign of weakness, they are a sign of compassion.

Julia Gillard is strong, smart and caring in her work to ensure a fairer, safer world.

There was that time a *powerful* young AFL player

TAYLA HARRIS

called out online trolls and misogynists

who sexualised and demeaned her

for *doing her job*.

And she showed those trolls exactly how strong she is and how a traditionally male-dominated sport is no longer just a club for boys. It's for everyone.

And she inspired many other women and men – players and fans, groundskeepers and CEOs – to speak out against misogyny and aggression towards women that hides behind an internet handle.

And now this strong athlete and her high, powerful kick are immortalised in bronze in AFL's heartland: Federation Square, Melbourne. For all to see.

Tayla Harris is a forward for the Carlton Football Club and a professional boxer. She was named 2021 Victorian Young Australian of the Year and is an ambassador for Our Watch, which works to prevent violence against women and children.

She showed the world that when women fight back against vile comments posted about them, they can win.

She reminded us that women do not have to stay quiet.

Tayla Harris is a world-class athlete who flies high for all the women who aspire to be just like her.

Feeling inspired? Remember:

Other people's comfort is not your responsibility.

There was that time an extraordinary artist

CHLOÉ HAYDEN

decided to *define her*

own happily ever after.

And she wrote a book about how being different was a superpower.

And about how nothing ever changes by staying the same.

And her voice was confident and honest and funny.

And she called on people to embrace their 'eye sparkles', and in doing so, she is helping create a culture of acceptance, validation and pride.

Chloé Hayden is an artist, author, neurodiversity advocate and actor whose storytelling has resonated with audiences worldwide.

She advocates for more diverse storytelling to help inspire and unite everyone.

She encourages neurodivergent people to be themselves, and not feel required to mask their true selves in public, including stimming. Her storytelling as an actor has resonated with audiences worldwide.

Chloé Hayden is brave and brilliant.

Illustrated by
Selin Ala

There was that time

EMMA HORN

made TikTok a *safe place*

for queer kids.

And she spoke as an unapologetically queer person about her lived experiences.

And she gave a voice to young queer girls, reminding us during our darkest moments that there's a happier, colourful light at the end of the tunnel. Never mind the moment she asked her mum who she'd rather date: Ruby Rose or Kristen Stewart?

And she showed us that it's okay to be fluid and confident – and it's okay if that changes and then changes again.

Emma Horn is many things in many spheres. She is an actor, a writer, a TikTok sensation, a creator of humorous, educational content, an LGBTQIA+ influencer – and more.

She celebrates her uniqueness and inspires others to explore their own journey on their own terms.

Emma Horn wants you to live your best life, the best way you know how.

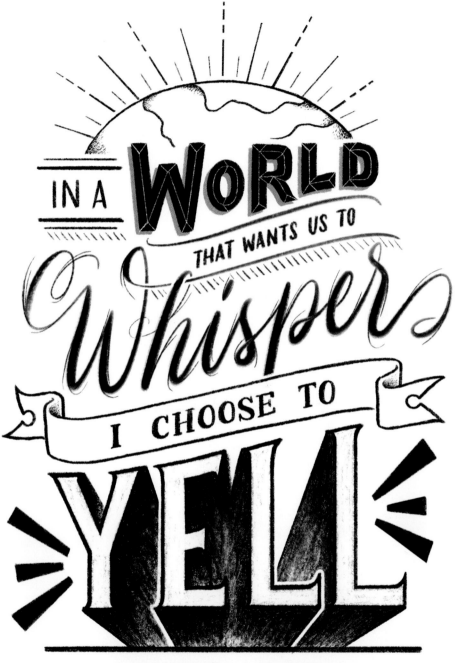

IN A WORLD THAT WANTS US TO Whisper I CHOOSE TO YELL

LUVVIE AJAYI

There was that time

JAMEELA JAMIL

wasn't afraid to take on influencers who endorse diet and detox products that are potentially harmful and dangerous.

And her petition on change.org to stop celebrities from promoting these products on social media gained more than 240,000 signatures.

And her campaign worked, convincing global companies such as Facebook and Instagram to change their policies around diet and detox products being shown to minors.

And Jameela's activism didn't stop there.

Jameela Jamil is a British former TV presenter whose breakout Hollywood acting role was in the hit show *The Good Place*. Jameela started @i_weigh, which began as an Instagram account focusing on body positivity and has grown into a community platform whose mission is to 'amplify, advocate, and pass the mic' for all kinds of diverse and under-represented voices.

She earned her fair share of haters as she spoke out about issues such as eating disorder culture, mental health, disability, reproductive rights, feminism and toxic media pile-ons of women in the public eye.

She doesn't let that stop her from continuing to speak up, to learn, to be an ally and to call out toxic culture wherever she sees it.

Jameela Jamil is unfiltered, unapologetic and unstoppable.

There was that time a journalist

ANTOINETTE LATTOUF

looked up at five different TV screens showing breakfast news and realised that none of the presenters on the screens looked like her . . . or like anyone else in her vicinity in the Sydney suburban gym.

And she said that it was ridiculous, and things had to change.

And she started Media Diversity Australia to help create a media landscape that looks and sounds like multicultural Australia. And in doing so she raised the eyebrows of those who felt that media accountability, representation and transparent reportability was not necessary.

And she lost some (bad) friendships and was constantly rebuked for rocking the boat.

And she stayed true to herself, and to the cause, because a diverse editorial team makes for better journalism and a better democracy. And because she knew it was just and she knew it was right.

Antoinette Lattouf is a broadcaster, columnist and mental-health ambassador.

She is the author of *How to Lose Friends and Influence White People*.

She is a champion for diverse and inclusive workplaces and is not afraid to speak up about discrimination.

She has called out racism from a young age, even when the conversations were uncomfortable and the backlash cruel and unfair.

She has always been frank, fearless and funny.

Antoinette Lattouf shows us that we can tackle tricky issues with humour and heart and that we all have a role to play to make society better and fairer.

Illustrated by
Jessica Cruickshank

Don't avoid

CONFLICT

AT ALL COSTS.

You are your own

BEST ADVOCATE.

There was that time
a talented young performer

JENNIFER LOPEZ

refused to be *pigeonholed*.

And when she was told she should stick to dancing, she started to act too.

And when she was told she should stick to acting, she started to sing too.

And then she did all three and was called a 'diva', where male counterparts with similar skills would be called a 'triple threat'.

And she kept working and striving, and eventually she took over the entertainment world, becoming a global icon for strength, determination, hard work and humanity. She showed her daughter and a generation of daughters that they can strive to be as many things as they want to be – and that hard work can be done by anyone, from any background.

Jennifer Lopez grew up in The Bronx, New York City. She started working as a kid and has never stopped. She is self-made and has built her life around hard work and determination.

She is a megawatt-shining example of never, ever letting anyone tell you not to follow your dreams.

Jennifer Lopez is Jenny from the Block, she is JLo, she is whatever and whoever she chooses to be.

There was that time a woman

MEGHAN MARKLE

prioritised her mental health over the expectations of an entire country – and she still hasn't heard the end of it.

And she stood firm and said she would not allow herself to be silenced and controlled – instead, she removed herself from the situation to start afresh for herself and her family.

And she used her position to continue her long-standing charity work and advocacy for women's rights and social justice on a global scale.

And she showed the world how to withstand public condemnation with grace and strength.

Meghan Markle is a mother, an actor, an author, a duchess, a feminist and an advocate.

She married one of the most famous men in the world and became a duchess, but she refused to let her title and position eclipse her.

She has been a global ambassador for World Vision Canada, penned an op-ed for *TIME* magazine concerning stigma surrounding women's menstrual health and advocated for the United Nations Entity for Gender Equality and the Empowerment of Women.

She marked her fortieth birthday by launching 40x40, a campaign that asks people around the world to spend 40 minutes of their time mentoring women who are re-entering the workforce.

Meghan Markle is strong, smart and she isn't going anywhere.

Stop saying yes to everything.

There was that time a young English woman

GINA MARTIN

was 'upskirted', and she

fought back.

And she kept fighting and fighting, lobbying the government to #StopSkirtingTheIssue until the practice – the epitome of gender inequality, because how many men wear skirts in public social settings? – was made illegal in England and Wales.

And as she campaigned she endured sexist, misogynist and violent threats from men online.

And she showed us that one person can make a difference if they don't give up.

Gina Martin is a writer, public speaker and campaigner who advocates for equal rights for all.

She fought to create the *Voyeurism (Offences) Act 2019* and then campaigned successfully to change Instagram's global policy on nudity to stop discrimination against women based on body shape and size.

She encourages people to advocate for what they believe in.

She is a stylist and a disrupter.

Gina Martin believes in not stopping until you make a difference.

There was that time

CHANEL MILLER

relinquished her anonymity and *refused*

to be known only as a sexual-assault victim.

And she channelled her anger to expose the realities of a justice system that protects perpetrators of sexual assault rather than its victims.

And her victim statement went viral, sparking international outrage at her offender's lax sentencing; and a call to action with hundreds of women sharing their own stories.

And she transformed her trauma into art. Into strength. Into healing. Her profoundly moving memoir, *Know My Name*, received critical claim for its courage, power and importance.

Chanel Miller is more than a survivor. She is more than her trauma. She is an artist. A writer. A public speaker.

She was Glamour 2016 and 2019's Woman of the Year and helped spark the #MeToo movement.

She is fierce, resilient and compassionate in her quest to embolden and validate the very real experiences of sexual assault.

Chanel Miller is reclaiming her story and her identity.

Feeling inspired? Remember:

You are good enough exactly as you are.

There was that time

KEMI NEKVAPIL

decided to make it her life's

mission to encourage women to

step into their own power.

And being English-born with a Nigerian heritage, she felt she had to prove her worth as a 'good black girl' while being raised by five sets of white foster parents.

And she decided to own her story and inspire others to break down the cultural myths around asking and worthiness.

And she refused to limit herself to someone else's idea of what her life should look like.

Kemi Nekvapil is an author and leadership coach with a decade of experience and thirty years of personal and professional development. Before she went on to inspire thousands of women, she trained as a baker, taught yoga and worked with the Royal Shakespeare Company.

She steps into her power.

She practises presence.

She takes responsibility for her story.

Kemi Nekvapil challenges us to lead empowered lives.

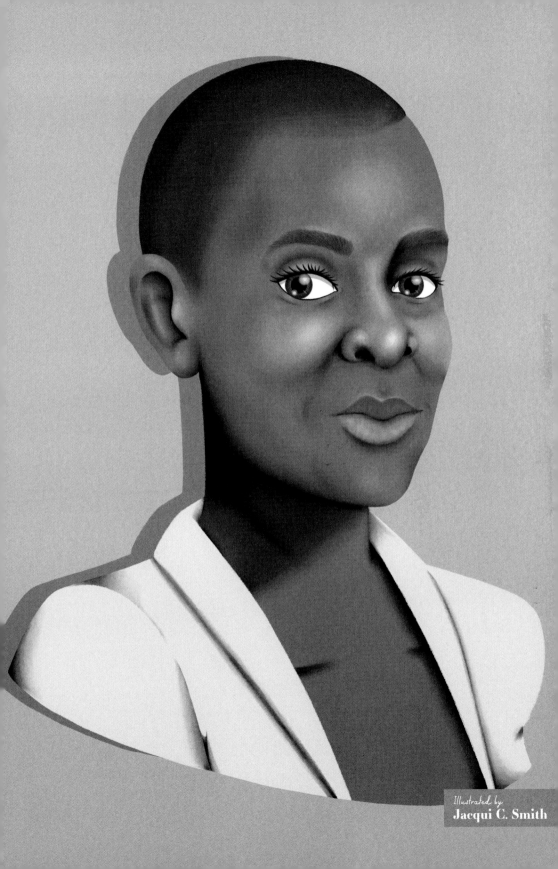

There was that time a little girl from America

MICHELLE OBAMA

showed what women can do

when *they don't give up*.

And when, at age five, she got the wrong answer in class, she demanded a do-over. She wasn't prepared to settle.

And as she grew, she used that fire to embody 'Princeton material', which her guidance counsellor told her she would never be. She was.

And her life became a pursuit for unprejudiced and available education for girls. Girls who are hardworking and bright but denied the simplest of rights. Through many and varied initiatives, she encouraged women not to see her as the US First Lady, but as a girl from the South Side of Chicago who will never stop fighting to give them a voice. To give them access and equity. Gifts that can be taken for granted by those who never have to ask for them.

Michelle Obama is a lawyer, a mother, the first African-American First Lady of the United States, and author of inspirational memoirs *Becoming* and *The Light We Carry*.

She has dedicated her life and career to representing minority groups and helping individuals overcome self-doubt and achieve success, particularly young women who endure harrowing circumstances just to go to school safely.

She is a born leader who, through campaigns such as Get Her There and Let Girls Learn, shows these girls with big ambitions that it's okay to struggle, but not without a fight.

Michelle Obama is an incorrigible advocate for surviving the odds.

SPEAK YOUR Mind even if your VOICE shakes

MAGGIE KUHN

There was that time

ALEXANDRIA OCASIO-CORTEZ

became the youngest woman elected to the
United States Congress, and she *refused* to back
down to the most powerful men in government.

And she was called a 'firebrand' and was criticised for the way she pronounced her own name and was accused of faking her arrest, highlighting the higher level of scrutiny women, and particularly Hispanic women, in positions of power face every day.

And still, she protested and marched and argued and used her youth and smarts to empower future generations of activists.

And the hostility thrown her way from political opponents did not stop or silence her. Not for a day. Not even for a moment. She refused to be quiet, to 'play nice' like so many women and girls before her have been told to.

Alexandria Ocasio-Cortez worked as a waitress and bartender before she ran for Congress in 2018.

She advocates for those whose voices cannot be heard.

She stands up and speaks out for what she believes in.

Alexandria Ocasio-Cortez is a powerhouse and a role model.

There was that time a young social entrepreneur

NADYA OKAMOTO

broke the taboo and spoke publicly about periods.

And she advocated loudly against the menstrual inequities that see girls and women punished for bleeding every month.

And she posted images and videos of herself using tampons and pads and owning the fact that she has a menstrual cycle and that it's totally normal.

And she wasn't embarrassed or uncomfortable talking about these things, as girls are expected to be. She shouted out loud that having your period isn't weird or gross.

Nadya Okamoto wants girls' experiences with their periods to feel powerful and dignified, and for everyone – female and male – to have a greater understanding of how menstrual cycles work.

In 2016 at age sixteen, she founded an organisation called PERIOD, whose mission is to end period poverty and the stigma surrounding this inherently natural experience.

In 2018 at age twenty-one, she wrote a book about periods called *Period Power: A Manifesto for the Menstrual Movement*.

In 2020 at age twenty-three, she founded August, a lifestyle brand that creates products to help women manage their periods.

She is an entrepreneur, an author, an advocate and a leader.

Nadya Okamoto is determined to break down taboos and bring back period power.

Illustrated by
Kristina Rodriguez

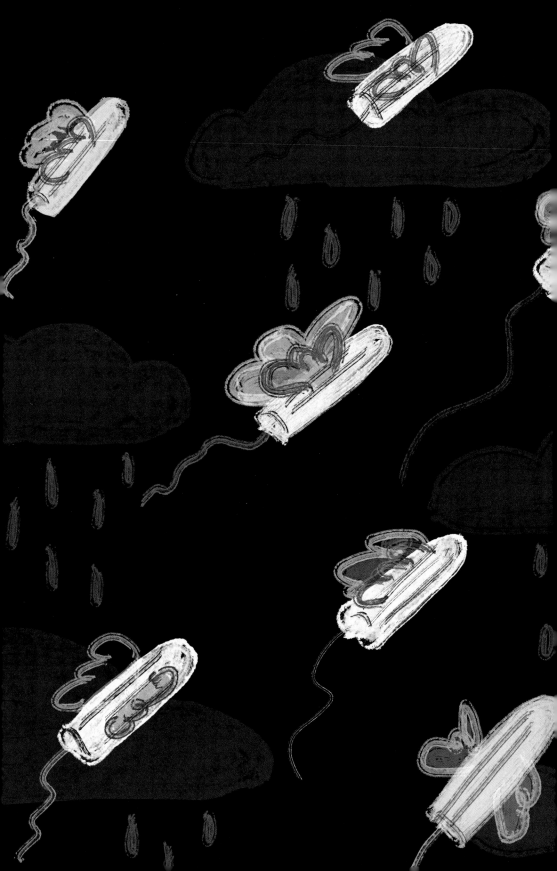

August 2022

Scotland is the first country in the world to make period products free.

Menstrual products such as tampons and sanitary pads are available free of charge to 'anyone who needs them'. (parliament.scot) The bill was introduced by Monica Lennon MSP. Under it, period products will be freely available at schools, colleges and other public spaces as well as delivered to those who require them.

There was that time an engineer
and marathon runner

TURIA PITT

refused to die.

And after she suffered burns to sixty-five percent of her body while running an ultramarathon in the Western Australian desert, her family was told she would not survive.

And she fought to live and prove everyone wrong. She refused to listen to the people who told her all the things she would never be able to do.

And she learned to walk again. She learned to run again. She defied all the doubters and showed us what is possible with self-belief and hard work.

Turia Pitt has completed marathons and ultramarathons and an IRONMAN competition. She has built a career as an author and motivational speaker and run coach, and given birth to two children – and much, much more.

She established the RUN with Turia program to help women learn to run and experience the joy and empowerment of achieving something they didn't think was possible.

She will not be told what she cannot do. She does it anyway.

Turia Pitt is resilient, enduring and determined to live her best life and help others live theirs.

There was that time a young actor

FLORENCE PUGH

refused to be ashamed of her body.

And she was insulted and demeaned and judged as she walked the red carpet in a haute couture sheer pink tulle dress.

And she refused to cower, to show embarrassment or awkwardness. She owned her decision to wear a transparent dress, and hit back against the critics who tried to make her feel ashamed of her size and shape. '#f—ingfreethef—ingnipple,' she said, instead.

And she talked about being raised by strong women who taught her to be comfortable in herself, in taking up space. To not go along with the conditioning that tells girls to be small, to shrink themselves so as not to be too loud, too seen. Florence is loud and seen and a shining star.

Florence Pugh is a British actor who has worked in everything from Shakespeare to the Marvel Multiverse. She shares stories about women who refuse to be silenced.

She is proud of her body and her mind.

She shows young women what they can do.

Florence Pugh is bright, successful and comfortable in her own skin.

Illustrated by
Adele Leyris

Feeling inspired? Remember:

Kindness is always cool.

There was that time a thirteen-year-old
Australian environmental activist

IZZY RAJ-SEPPINGS

made global headlines for *fighting*

for what she believes in.

And she was photographed with tears streaming down her face as she stared down riot police who threatened to arrest her at a climate protest outside the prime minister's residence following devastating bushfires – but she wouldn't budge.

And as she was moved on by the riot police, she held her sign high:

> LOOK AT WHAT YOU'VE LEFT US
> WATCH US FIGHT IT
> WATCH US WIN.

And it was the start of something much bigger. In 2021 she led a crowd of 10,000 in a 'School Strike 4 Climate' protest march through central Sydney and was one of eight teenagers who brought a class action lawsuit against the federal government, leading to a landmark ruling that the federal environment minister has a moral obligation to children to consider the harm caused by climate change.

Izzy Raj-Seppings is a brave and committed activist who fights for an urgent and more effective response to the climate crisis.

She continues to keep the pressure on the country's decision makers through protests, social media, public appearances – any action that can make a difference.

Izzy Raj-Seppings is articulate, determined and passionate in her fight for a better, safer future for her country and the world.

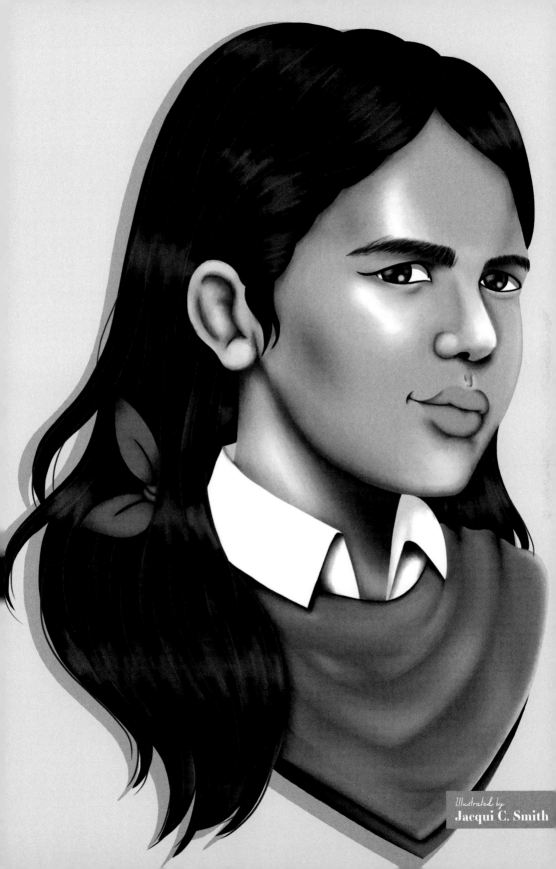

There was that time

RIHANNA

was *asked* by a reporter what she

was looking for in a man – and *had the*

perfect response.

And she replied, 'Pardon? I'm not looking for a man. Let's start there.'

And her clapback showed up the question for what it was: presumptuous, and relying on the tedious assumption that a woman must be looking to be in a (hetero, monogamous) coupling.

And it was one of many now-famous clapbacks from the musician, including shutting down journalists for misogynistic comments about her body shape, hair and fashion choices.

There was that other time **Rihanna** made history with her cosmetics line that featured a 40-shade range of foundations, making it one of the most inclusive beauty brands globally.

And all those other times her fashion line has celebrated play, dance and free movement in a way that reclaims women's bodies as their own, rather than submitting to the 'male gaze'.

Rihanna is a musical artist and businesswoman. She has received nine Grammy awards and is the second-highest-selling female musical artist of all time. Her charity, the Clara Lionel Foundation, focuses on closing poverty and education gaps for girls, and climate resilience and climate justice.

Feeling inspired? Remember:

You can laugh at yourself and still feel good.

There was that time a young
rugby league star

JULIA ROBINSON

refused to be told that

her body was wrong.

And she called out the online abusers who said she was built like a man and her muscles were too big and they made her less appealing.

And through her refusal to be ashamed of her physique, she showed that being strong and powerful is equally empowering for women and men.

And she drew attention to the culture of online trolling of sportswomen who compete – and succeed – in sports traditionally dominated by men. She showed that it cannot be tolerated, and it takes men and women to speak up and speak out to change the status quo.

Julia Robinson has been part of three premiership-winning teams for the Brisbane Broncos. She is an elite athlete whose conduct on and off the field inspires the next generation of league players, regardless of their gender.

She is not willing to let the insults hurt her or abusive strangers define her.

Julia Robinson is strong, powerful and proud.

There was that time an artist and
proud Pitjantjatjara woman

SALLY SCALES

used her voice and art

to inspire change.

And she encouraged First Nations peoples to participate
in decision-making about laws and policies affecting their
communities via the Uluru Statement from the Heart.

And she spoke about Voice, Treaty and Makarrata (coming together
after struggle) while leading a First Nations art collective, and
collaborated with clothing brands to create Uluru Statement,
Voice and Makarrata artwork to spread the word.

And she also supports other artists and women, highlighting the
need for Voice, Treaty and Truth.

Sally Scales is the youngest person (and second woman) elected
as Chairperson of the APY Executive Board. She has worked with
the APY Art Centre Collective since 2013 in cultural liaison, elder
support and spokesperson roles and is a consultant for the Art
Gallery of South Australia.

She is part of the youth leadership team for the Uluru Statement
reform, and has been involved in the Referendum Council's
Constitution regional dialogues in Ross River, Adelaide and the
national convention in Uluru. Since then Sally has been involved
with leadership for Voice, Treaty and Truth.

Sally Scales is a talented, passionate leader who proudly represents
First Nations peoples and creates art to inspire all Australians.

Accept the CREDIT & PRAISE you've earned. you're Extraordinary.

There was that time a musician

TAYLOR SWIFT

decided to *stop playing nice.*

And she spoke out about the unfairness of the music industry and about being prevented from having a say in who owned her music.

And instead of accepting that her first six albums belonged to someone else – instead of resigning herself to the fact that the songs based on her own experiences couldn't belong to her, songs she had written and shared with millions on stages across the globe, songs that had won her twelve Grammy awards – she went into the studio and rerecorded her masters.

Taylor Swift is one of the most popular musicians of all time, with an estimated 114 million records sold. She has released ten studio albums and won countless awards across music genres.

She is also known for her philanthropic efforts and her line of sustainable clothing in collaboration with Stella McCartney.

She reminds us that we can take credit for our own work. We can be loud in our own house.

She isn't afraid to try new things, isn't afraid to fail, and shows us that self-truth is the most important truth.

Taylor Swift is talented, successful and unafraid to stand up for herself.

Illustrated by
Rebecca King

There was that time a young woman

GRACE TAME

refused to smile.

And she was called disrespectful and ungracious and childish.

And so she eloquently reminded us all that it is through submissive smiles and self-defeating surrenders that abuse culture is allowed to survive and thrive. And this must be discussed and stopped.

And the public criticism she received for behaving in a perfectly civil but not gregarious manner epitomised the unfair expectations placed on girls and women to be friendly and hospitable regardless of how they feel.

Grace Tame was Australian of the Year in 2021, recognised for her advocacy for survivors of sexual assault. This advocacy – including the #LetHerSpeak campaign – led to Tasmanian law reform, which had previously prohibited sexual abuse survivors from publicly identifying themselves or speaking about their experiences.

She established The Grace Tame Foundation, which strives for cultural and structural change to eradicate sexual abuse of children.

She is not willing to tolerate civility for the sake of civility.

Grace Tame is brave, uncompromising and compassionate in her advocacy.

Illustrated by
Janelle Burger

There was that time a queer child of immigrants

MARIA THATTIL

became Miss Universe Australia and

broke the mould that says you can

only be one thing.

And shortly after winning the title in 2020, she started advocating fiercely for social causes and speaking up about her experiences of racism, homophobia and other toxic behaviours.

And she didn't abide commentary that suggested she was 'only' a model. She called out the hecklers and built a life around the things that are important to her, to help others.

Maria Thattil is a writer, TV presenter, actor and public speaker. She is the author of *Unbounded* and the founder of the *BEING HUMAN with Maria Thattil* podcast. She holds degrees in Psychology and Management, is a member of the United Nations Association of Australia and an ongoing ambassador for Minus 18 Youth and The Ovarian Cancer Research Foundation.

She champions projects that work to stamp out racism and sexism, and foster inclusivity, representation, positive mental health and youth empowerment.

Maria Thattil is an inspiration; a rising (multifaceted) star.

Illustrated by
Adele Leyris

There was that time a Swedish teenager

GRETA THUNBERG

skipped school to protest climate change –

and *changed the world.*

And she inspired kids to join her in Stockholm and around the globe, pressuring governments to do something concrete to combat climate change – not in the next few decades, but now.

And she was criticised and ridiculed by some very powerful men, because she was just a kid and she was a bit 'different' and what would she know?

And she refused to be treated like a naughty child. Instead, she built a movement and spoke with world leaders and at international meetings such as the UN Climate Action Summit where she held adults to account. She would not let them fail future generations.

Greta Thunberg continues her work to address the effects of climate change on our planet.

She does not back down to powerful people, and she embraces her Asperger's Syndrome, her 'difference', her 'superpower'.

She has mobilised a generation of engaged young people to stand up for what they believe in and agitate for their future. This has become known as 'the Greta effect'.

Greta Thunberg is a beacon of hope and a powerful force for positive change.

Hate public speaking?

Heaps of us do. Here are some tips on speaking up with confidence (even if you really don't want to).

Be prepared!

Even the most confident smartypants speaker knows to prep ahead of time. Jot down some notes, read them through and practise your speech on a willing guinea pig. Then, even if you want to come across as casual and unprepared, you'll know your stuff.

Go first!

Just get it over with, whether you're in a classroom, at work or enduring an awkward family occasion. Challenge yourself to raise your hand or speak up – you'll be glad you did.

Breathe deeply.

Taking long, slow, controlled breaths can help slow your heart rate, which basically tricks your body into thinking you're not as nervous as you really are.

Just be you.

Don't try to find a fancier way to say what you want to say. If your words feel true to who you are, they will be understood.

Start small.

If the thought of standing up in front a group bigger than your parents makes you want to run away, try something same-but-different on a smaller scale: hum a song in public or chat to a stranger in a queue. Realising it's not that bad will help you take bigger steps. IDK, maybe just vent about a micro-injustice at yourself in the mirror to fire yourself up beforehand!

There was that time a young Kamilaroi woman

CHEREE TOKA

wanted the Aboriginal flag to *fly*
above the Sydney Harbour Bridge.

And she led a campaign to make it happen.

And she was told it was not flag protocol; it would be too expensive; she needed community support. So, she started a petition and crowdsourced the funds despite the racism and setbacks the campaign faced.

And it took five tough years but finally she gained 177,000 signatures as well as the support of politicians including a premier and a prime minister, and the second flag on the bridge was replaced – permanently – by the Aboriginal one.

And thanks to Cheree's perseverance, passion, leadership and advocacy, in 2022, First Nations peoples can look above the bridge and feel the same sense of belonging as non-Indigenous people and see a symbol of unity, respect and reconciliation.

Now, all Australian people can look at the bridge and see the true history of their country acknowledged.

Cheree Toka is a proud Kamilaroi woman and activist.

She is known for her fight for First Nations inclusion and recognition, and as a businesswoman running a First Nations owned company.

She was not willing to stand by and see First Nations art, culture and icons not displayed or represented in public spaces.

Cheree Toka is a leader and inspiration for First Nations people and all people in Australia.

There was that time a champion tennis player

SERENA WILLIAMS

got angry on the court in one of the

biggest matches of her career.

And instead of respect, and an ear, she got a penalty as she accused the chair umpire of treating her more harshly than her male counterparts.

And her anger was described by the media as a 'hissy fit' and as 'a meltdown' and as 'hysterical' – terms not used to describe men's reactions and emotions.

And by standing up for herself and her valid emotions and actions, she broke the rules women are often told to play by: don't be too strong, don't be too loud, don't express yourself, don't be angry.

Serena Williams is one of the greatest tennis players of all time.

She has won four Olympic gold medals and holds 23 Grand Slam singles, as well as 14 titles in women's doubles with her sister Venus, and two in mixed doubles.

She is a UNICEF Goodwill Ambassador and works for numerous charities including The Serena Williams Fund.

Serena Williams is strong, sure and unapologetic.

I REALLY THINK A CHAMPION IS DEFINED NOT BY THEIR WINS BUT BY HOW THEY CAN Recover WHEN THEY FALL.

Serena Williams

There was that time an activist

VARSHA YAJMAN

demanded Australia

do better for the climate.

And she joined the Australian Youth Climate Coalition's leadership program when she was in high school. She learned how she could make a difference, letting her voice be heard at gatherings and panels, and speaking out on a nationally televised TV program alongside politicians.

And she helped organise 350,000 students for School Strike for Climate, sharing her views on radio and in newspapers, magazines and TV interviews.

And these efforts meant that an anti-climate politician was voted out and student voices were taken seriously by politicians and the wider community.

Varsha Yajman is a speaker, podcaster and advocate for climate justice and mental health awareness.

She is a coordinator at SAPNA South Asian Climate Solidarity and co-host of a podcast, *Not to be Controversial*, aiming to create a community for young South Asians to feel represented and empowered. She works for a legal firm conducting climate change litigation.

Varsha Yajman works to bring people together and make systemic change.

There was that time an
eleven-year-old Pakistani girl

MALALA YOUSAFZAI

was told by the Taliban that she could no longer

attend school, and she *refused to stay silent.*

Instead, she spoke out and became a target.

And one day when Malala was fifteen, a member of the Taliban boarded a bus she was on, and shot her in the head because of the things she had been saying.

And she lived.

And she continued her education.

And she spoke out, showing girls everywhere that they do matter, that they are entitled to an education and a future of their choosing.

Malala Yousafzai was the youngest ever recipient of the Nobel Peace Prize – in 2014 when she was seventeen.

She worked alongside her activist father to establish the Malala Fund, which aims to raise awareness and give every girl a chance to attend school.

She refused to back down even when her life was at risk, and she continues her fight for all the girls who come after her.

Malala Yousafzai is brave and compassionate and unstoppable.

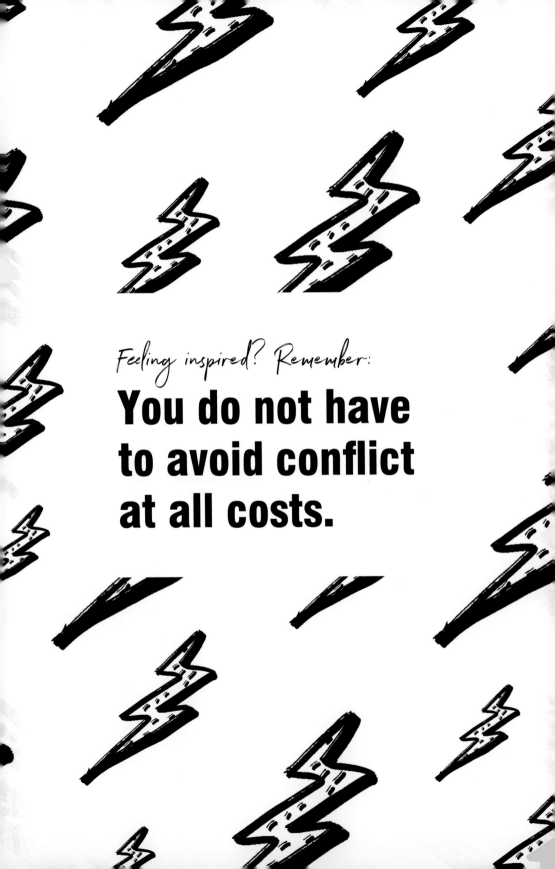

Feeling inspired? Remember:

You do not have to avoid conflict at all costs.

There was that time a young, immensely talented, popular performer

ZENDAYA

called out a teen magazine that Photoshopped her body to make her look slimmer.

And she released the original and retouched images side-by-side on social media so her followers could see the real her.

And the magazine apologised. But the problem still permeates every facet of girls' online lives, and it takes strong role models to lead the way to show girls that they do not have to buy into the idea of the 'perfect', 'acceptable' body.

Zendaya is a successful musician, a model, an actor and a style icon for young women everywhere.

She uses her public profile to hold the media – and wider society – to account over the unrealistic and dangerous body-image expectations they promote for girls.

She speaks up for herself and for other women against racial slurs, Hollywood colourism and body-shamers, sharing her attempts to teach aggressors rather than continue the cycle of attack, knowing that the best way forward might be different each time, but honesty and self-love are always the right path.

Zendaya does not sit quietly and watch injustice.

There was that time a female filmmaker

CHLOÉ ZHAO

took on a man's world and made it

beautiful for us all.

And she showed the boundary-crossing beauty a film can possess when created by an outsider.

And she explored the lived experiences of outsiders, sparking conversation and seeking understanding and empathy.

And she was bold in the 'man's world' of filmmaking.

Chloé Zhao is a Chinese-born filmmaker who explores an array of cinema, from independent films to the Marvel Multiverse.

She won Academy Awards for best film and best director for her work on *Nomadland*.

She shows us that femininity is a strength and that people of all genders can embrace so-called 'feminine' attributes.

Chloé Zhao utilises her skill and passion to share female stories.

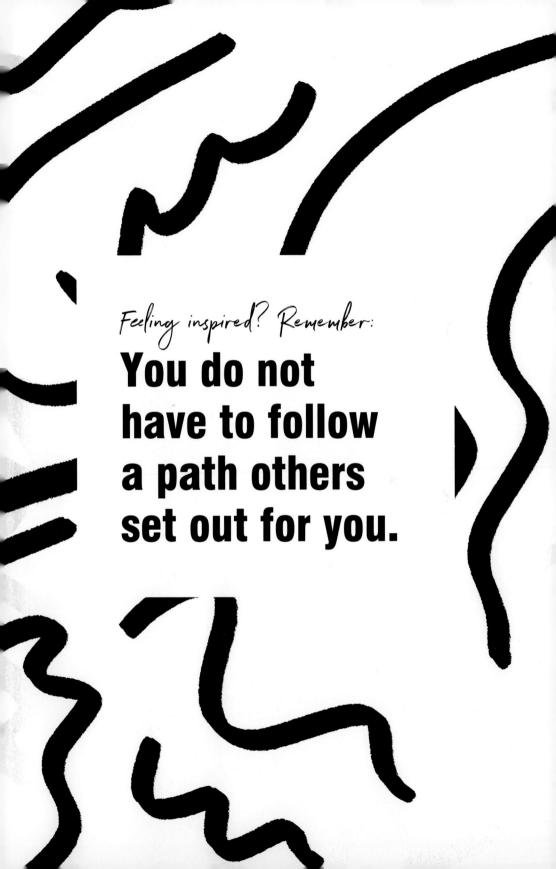

Feeling inspired? Remember:

You do not have to follow a path others set out for you.

IT'S **OKAY** TO BE

ANNOYED CRANKY SALTY PISSED **ANGRY.**

Meet the Illustrators

Selin Ala is a Sydney-based illustrator who blends watercolour and pencil to create her distinctive, realistic style. Her favourite subjects range from portraits to landscapes, with a special place in her heart for animals, especially her cats. Through her art, she aims to capture the essence of her subjects while maintaining the loose, organic quality of her mediums and techniques.

Janelle Barone is a Melbourne-based artist and digital illustrator, creating immersive illustrations for a range of editorial and commercial clients. Janelle has a folio full of solid colour, subtle gradients and strong lighting that never fails to capture a unique mood.

Janelle Burger is an Indigenous Australian (Noongar) and Italian illustrator based in Paris. Her work is influenced by pop culture, fashion, video games and food. For Janelle, being connected to country and family is the most important thing. Being Noongar–Sicilian, Janelle feels joined to both cultures equally and even though she lives in another country, Janelle can create artworks from abroad and still feel connected. No matter where she is in the world, Janelle has a strong bond with Australia.

Kat Chadwick is a Melbourne-based artist with a love for the problem-solving involved in working to a brief. With a body of work that is all about energetic inky lines and solid colour, Kat offers a unique perspective on the often overlooked aspects of our everyday domestic lives.

Jessica Cruickshank is a master illustrator and designer best known for her captivating book covers using an innovative mix of hand-lettering combined with her energetic illustration style.

Sabrena Khadija is a DC-based, Sierra-Leonean American illustrator. As a Black Non-Binary creative, Sabrena takes pride in creating work that helps others feel seen and inspired. Not only to see beauty within themselves, but to recognise and acknowledge that of others. They are one of the growing number of human beings who seek inclusive and innovative spaces to explore art, creativity and joy in meaningful and impactful ways.

Rebecca King is a Sydney-based book designer and illustrator. She studied a BA in Illustration and has spent the past ten years creating fun, commercial books across Australia and the UK. She primarily digitally paints using a Wacom Cintiq, but likes to adapt the medium to suit the book. From recipe books to unicorn board books, she loves delving into a new project, bridging together design and illustration to create cohesive, visually striking books.

Mel Lane is an editor and illustrator based on Cammeraygal land in Sydney. Inspired by the intricate details and textures of everyday things, she creates nuanced pencil and digital illustrations of people, fashion and nature. She also has a Master's in Publishing and Communications from the University of Melbourne, and as a book editor has had the privilege of working with talented authors across fiction and non-fiction.

Emma Leonard is known for elegant fashion and botanical illustrations. Her work has graced everything from YA book covers to global beauty campaigns. By mixing pencil, watercolour and digital processes, her work celebrates the quieter moments in life through her warm colour palettes and flawless finish.

Adele Leyris is a Franco-English illustrator based in London. Inspired by nature and travel, her work is rooted in observational drawing and travel journalism, which can become anything from botanical compositions to landscapes and portraiture. But she particularly enjoys working on projects that are close to her values, which are feminism, animal protection, diversity and sustainable travel. She also has a passion for confronting antagonist notions such as using old and new techniques, like embroidery and augmented reality.

Tori-Jay Mordey is an Indigenous Australian illustrator and artist based in Meanjin (Brisbane). Tori-Jay works in digital illustration, traditional drawing, painting, printmaking, film and murals. Much of her work revolves around human connection and exploring her racial identity. She often combines stylistic cartoons with realism to help capture the complexities of human emotions, distorting and exaggerating the characters to express and expose their vulnerabilities. In her mural work, Tori-Jay strives to create visually playful imagery to softly embrace onlookers with colours, life and vibrancy.

Michelle Pereira is an illustrator who breathes new life into a range of characters and her own world through a calculated use of bold graphic texture and symbolism, elevating themes of inclusivity and the feminine.

Georgia Perry is an iconic Melbourne artist who makes feel-good illustrations that are all about spreading joy. With her own line of products and a range of commercial clients under her belt, Georgia brings an optimistic voice to each of her projects.

Kristina Rodriguez is a Miami-based illustrator of Cuban and Paraguayan background. She has a BFA in painting and sculpture from Florida International University, but her first love has always been drawing. Kristina works mostly digitally but always looks for ways to include traditional techniques and mediums in her projects. She loves colour, line, light and mood; and is inspired by traditional classical painting, expressionism, surrealism, mid-century graphic design and folk art. Kristina's work has been exhibited at Wolfsonian/FIU, MOCA and the Scope International Art Fair; and she has collaborated on multiple occasions with the New World Symphony.

Jacqui C. Smith creates unique artwork that showcases diversity among women of colour. A graduate of Columbia College of Chicago with a BA in Traditional Animation, Jacqui has created children's books and illustrations and sells her artwork at festivals, boutiques and galleries across the United States, and has created four colouring books. Jacqui believes there needs to be better treatment, representation and acceptance of women of colour, and hopes that her art serves as a reminder that they should not be overlooked.

Violet Tobacco is an illustrator based in Atlanta, Georgia. She studied theatre in college but gravitated toward other mediums of art before graduating. Always a storyteller with an affinity for whimsy, humour and a well-delivered moral, she is most fond of illustration as a means of expression. She enjoys working with other creative individuals to build stories that help us better understand who we are.

Acknowledgements

Not Here to Make You Comfortable celebrates the brave, awesome women who stand up, speak out and inspire change. In small ways, in big ways, in whatever way they can, they make the world a better place for themselves and for those who come after them.

We – the Young Readers team at Penguin Random House Australia – have been honoured to highlight fifty incredible women of all ages, backgrounds and experiences who have spent a moment or a lifetime doing what was right for them, which, in turn, motivates us all to live as authentically as we can. We had space for just fifty, but we hope this book serves as a starting point for you to keep searching and finding brave, unique women everywhere.

With thanks to our team of enthusiastic, skilled writers: Zoe Bechara, Lydia Burgham, Jessica de Caria, Claire de Medici, Vishali Seshadri, Amy Thomas, Mary Verney and Zoe Walton. And to Holly Toohey and Belinda Conners for invaluable input and enthusiasm.

We are also incredibly grateful to the talented illustrators who embraced this project and created beautiful artwork to bring our spotlighted women to visual life.

This book was made big, bold and beautiful by the incomparable talent of Rebecca King, our in-house designer whose style and skill made these women and their ideas stand out as they deserve to. Becca also brought images of Yassmin Abdel-Magied, Millie Bobby Brown, AJ Clementine and Taylor Swift to life in these pages. Caroline Lee, another shining designer on our team, contributed some amazing word art throughout the book. And Mel Lane, who spends her days editing books on our Adult list, contributed gorgeous portraits of Rachel Cusk, Chanel Miller and Chloé Zhao. What a lucky team we are!

Finally, we were excited and oh so grateful to have Illeana Hodge, Eva Hunstead and Isabel Hunstead – awesome young women and future game changers – share their insights and opinions from the teen trenches. Your passion for this project spurred us on to get it right; so, thank you!

Need help?

If you're going through a tough situation that you don't feel comfortable talking about with your friends or family, you can find help elsewhere. Reach out to a counsellor on a free anonymous hotline or website.

AUSTRALIA

Kids Helpline: 1800 55 1800 / kidshelpline.com.au

Free, private and confidential 24-hour phone and online counselling service for people aged 5 to 25. You can call any time, for any reason.

NEW ZEALAND

0800 What's Up: 0800 942 8787

Mon–Sun 11am–11pm / whatsup.co.nz

Free counselling helpline and webchat service for children and teenagers.

PENGUIN BOOKS

UK | USA | Canada | Ireland | Australia
India | New Zealand | South Africa | China

Penguin Random House Australia is part of the Penguin Random House group of companies
whose addresses can be found at global.penguinrandomhouse.com.

First published by Penguin Books, an imprint of Penguin Random House Australia Pty Ltd, in 2023

Cover and internal design by Rebecca King © Penguin Random House Australia Pty Ltd

Additional internal word art by Caroline Lee © Penguin Random House Australia Pty Ltd

Cover portraits:
Zendaya by Janelle Burger
Millie Bobby Brown by Rebecca King
Serena Williams by Michele Pereira
Taylor Swift by Rebecca King

Printed and bound in Malaysia

 A catalogue record for this
book is available from the
National Library of Australia

ISBN 978 1 76 134058 1

penguin.com.au

We at Penguin Random House Australia acknowledge that Aboriginal and Torres Strait Islander
peoples are the Traditional Custodians and the first storytellers of the lands on which we live and work.
We honour Aboriginal and Torres Strait Islander peoples' continuous connection to Country, waters, skies
and communities. We celebrate Aboriginal and Torres Strait Islander stories, traditions and living cultures;
and we pay our respects to Elders past and present.

Here are fifty times a woman did something brave.
Something disruptive. Something exceptional.

We saw them. And we were inspired to be more
confident and maybe a little bold.

It's time to **STOP** saying yes all the time.

It's time to **STOP** apologising all the time.

It's time to **STOP** avoiding conflict all the time.

It's time to be true to our emotions, whatever they are.

We're not here to make you comfortable.

We're here to celebrate being ourselves.

ISBN: 978-1-76134-058-1

9 781761 340581

penguin.com.au